Eduard Mörike

Die Historie von der schönen Lau
The story of the beautiful Lau

Eduard Mörike

Die Historie von der schönen Lau
The story of the beautiful Lau

mit Illustrationen von
with illustrations by
Dorothee Menzel

Edition Axel Menges

Wir danken dem Verlag C. H. Beck für die Genehmigung, die englische Übersetzung von Stan Foulkes aus der Publikation: Eduard Mörike, *Die Historie von der schönen Lau / The story of Lau, the beautiful water nymph*, hrsg. von Peter Schmid, Langewiesche-Brandt, jetzt Verlag C. H. Beck, zu übernehmen.

We thank Verlag C. H. Beck for the permission to use the English translation by Stan Foulkes from the publication: Eduard Mörike, *Die Historie von der schönen Lau / The story of Lau, the beautiful water nymph*, ed. by Peter Schmid, Langewiesche-Brandt, now Verlag C. H. Beck.

© 2014 Edition Axel Menges, Stuttgart / London
ISBN 978-3-936681-83-3

Alle Rechte vorbehalten, besonders die der Übersetzung in andere Sprachen.
All rights reserved, especially those of translation into other languages.

Druck und Bindearbeiten / Printing and binding: Graspo CZ, a.s., Zlín, Tschechische Republik / Czech Republic

Englische Übersetzung / English translation: Stan Foulkes
Lektorat / Editorial work: Dorothea Duwe
Design: Axel Menges

8	Die Nixe auf dem Grunde des Blautopfs
9	Der Nonnenhof
10	Die Nixe lauscht der Orgelmusik
12	Der Hirtenjunge im Labyrinth der Blautopfhöhle
16	Die Nixe mit ihren Kammerzofen
17	Die Nixe in ihrem Schlafgemach
18	Die Nixe entsteigt dem Brunnen
19	Das Geschenk der Nixe
20	Der Nonnenhof
24	Das erste Lachen der Nixe
25	Die Nixe in den Kleidern der Menschen
28	Die Nixe streift durch das Haus
29	Das Rusenschloß im Mondschein
36	Die Nixe schlingt ihre Perlenkette um die Leine des Lots
37	Das Klötzle Blei
40	Die Nixe wird zum Blautopf getragen
41	Die drei Zofen halten nach ihrer Herrin Ausschau
42	Die große Wasserstraße
43	Die Ankunft des Donaunix
44	Abschied der Nixe

8	The water nymph on the Blautopf bottom
9	The Nun's Inn
10	The water nymph listens to the organ music
12	The shepherd boy in the labyrinth of the Blautopf caves
16	The water nymph with her chamber maids
17	The water nymph in her bedchamber
18	The water nymph emerges from the well
19	The gift of the water nymph
20	The Nun's Inn
24	The water nymph laughs for the first time
25	The water nymph in human clothes
28	The water nymph wanders through the house
29	The Rusen castle by moonlight
36	The water nymph winds her pearl necklace round the plumb cord
37	The lump of lead
40	The water nymph is carried to the Blautopf
41	The three maids searching for their mistress
42	The great waterway
43	The Donaunix arrives
44	The water nymph's farewell

Im Schwabenlande, auf der Alb, bei dem Städtlein Blaubeuren, dicht hinter dem alten Mönchskloster, sieht man nächst einer jähen Felsenwand den großen runden Kessel einer wundersamen Quelle, der Blautopf genannt. Gen Morgen sendet er ein Flüsschen aus, die Blau, welche der Donau zufällt. Dieser Teich ist einwärts wie ein tiefer Trichter, sein Wasser von Farbe ganz blau, sehr herrlich, mit Worten nicht wohl zu beschreiben; wenn man es aber schöpft, sieht es ganz hell in dem Gefäß.

Zu unterst auf dem Grund saß ehmals eine Wasserfrau mit langen fließenden Haaren. Ihr Leib war allenthalben wie eines schönen, natürlichen Weibs, dies eine ausgenommen, daß sie zwischen den Fingern und Zehen eine Schwimmhaut hatte, blühweiß und zärter als ein Blatt vom Mohn. Im Städtlein ist noch heutzutag ein alter Bau, vormals ein Frauenkloster, hernach zu einer großen Wirtschaft eingerichtet, und hieß darum der Nonnenhof. Dort hing vor sechzig Jahren noch ein Bildnis von dem Wasserweib, trotz Rauch und Alter noch wohl kenntlich in den Farben. Da hatte sie die Hände kreuzweis auf die Brust gelegt, ihr Angesicht sah weißlich, das Haupthaar schwarz, die Augen aber, welche sehr groß waren, blau. Beim Volk hieß sie die arge Lau im Topf, auch wohl die schöne Lau. Gegen die Menschen erzeigte sie sich bald böse, bald gut. Zuzeiten, wenn sie im Unmut den Gumpen übergehen ließ, kam Stadt und Kloster in Gefahr, dann brachten ihr die Bürger in einem feierlichen Aufzug oft Geschenke, sie zu begütigen, als: Gold- und Silbergeschirr, Becher, Schalen, kleine Messer und andre Dinge; dawider zwar, als einen heidnischen Gebrauch und Götzendienst, die Mönche redlich eiferten, bis derselbe auch endlich ganz abgestellt worden. So feind darum die Wasserfrau dem Kloster war, geschah es doch nicht selten, wenn Pater Emeran die Orgel drüben schlug und kein Mensch in der Nähe war, daß sie am lichten Tag mit halbem Leib heraufkam und zuhorchte; dabei trug sie zuweilen einen Kranz von breiten Blättern auf dem Kopf und auch dergleichen um den Hals.

Ein frecher Hirtenjung belauschte sie einmal in dem Gebüsch und rief: »Hei, Laubfrosch! git's guat Wetter?« Geschwinder als ein Blitz und giftiger als eine Otter fuhr sie heraus, ergriff den Knaben beim Schopf und riß ihn mit hinunter in eine ihrer nassen Kammern, wo sie den ohnmächtig gewordenen jämmerlich verschmachten und verfaulen lassen wollte. Bald aber kam er wieder zu sich, fand eine Tür und kam, über Stufen und Gänge, durch viele Gemächer in einen schönen Saal. Hier war es lieblich, glusam mitten im Winter. In einer Ecke brannte, indem die Lau und ihre Dienerschaft schon schlief, auf einem hohen Leuchter mit goldenen Vogelfüßen als Nachtlicht eine Ampel. Es stand viel köstlicher Hausrat herum an den Wänden, und diese waren samt dem Estrich ganz mit Teppichen staffiert, Bildweberei in allen Farben. Der Knabe hurtig nahm das Licht herunter von dem Stock, sah sich in Eile um, was er noch sonst erwischen mochte, und griff aus einem Schrank etwas heraus, das stak in einem Beutel und war mächtig schwer, deswegen er vermeinte, es sei Gold; lief dann und kam vor ein erzenes Pförtlein, das mochte in der Dicke gut zwo Fäuste sein, schob die Riegel zurück und stieg eine steinerne Treppe hinauf in unterschiedlichen Absätzen, bald links, bald wieder rechts, gewiß vierhundert Stufen, bis sie zuletzt ausgingen und er auf ungeräumte Klüfte stieß; da mußte er das Licht dahinten lassen und kletterte so mit Gefahr seines Lebens noch eine Stunde lang im Finstern hin und her, dann aber brachte er den Kopf auf einmal aus der Erde. Es war tief Nacht, und dicker Wald um ihn. Als er nach vielem Irregehen endlich mit der ersten Morgenhelle auf gänge Pfade kam und von dem Felsen aus das Städtlein unten erblickte, verlangte ihn am Tag zu sehen, was in dem Beutel wäre; da war es weiter nichts als ein Stück Blei, ein schwerer Kegel, spannenlang, mit einem Ohr an seinem obern Ende, weiß vor Alter. Im Zorn warf er den Plunder weg, ins Tal hinab, und sagte nachher wetter niemand von dem Raub, weil er sich dessen schämte. Doch kam von ihm die erste Kunde von der Wohnung der Wasserfrau unter die Leute.

Nun ist zu wissen, daß die schöne Lau nicht hier am Ort zu Hause war; vielmehr war sie, als eine Fürstentochter, und zwar von Mutterseiten her halbmenschlichen Geblüts, mit einem alten Donaunix am Schwarzen Meer vermählt. Ihr Mann verbannte sie, darum, daß sie nur tote Kinder hatte. Das aber kam, weil sie stets traurig war, ohn einige besondere Ursach. Die Schwiegermutter hatte ihr geweissagt, sie möge eher nicht eines lebenden Kindes genesen, als bis sie fünfmal von Herzen gelacht haben würde. Beim fünften Male müßte etwas sein, das dürfe sie nicht wissen, noch auch der alte Nix. Es wollte aber damit niemals glücken, soviel auch ihre Leute deshalb Fleiß anwendeten; endlich da mochte sie der alte König ferner nicht an seinem Hofe leiden und sandte sie an diesen Ort, unweit der obern Donau, wo seine Schwester wohnte. Die Schwiegermutter hatte ihr zum Dienst und Zeitvertreib etliche Kammerzofen und Mägde mitgegeben, so muntere und kluge Madchen, als je auf Entenfüßen gingen (denn was von dem gemeinen Stamm der Wasserweiber ist, hat rechte Entenfüße); die zogen sie, pur für die Langeweile, sechsmal des Tages anders an – denn außerhalb dem Wasser ging sie in köstlichen Gewandern, doch barfuß –, erzählten ihr alte Ge-

In Swabia, on the Alb, near the little town of Blaubeuren, close behind the old monastery, you can see beside a sheer rock face the big round basin of a wondrous spring called the Blue Pool. A little river, the Blau, flows eastwards from it and joins the Danube. This pond is shaped like a deep funnel, its water is quite blue in colour, most lovely and difficult to describe in words. When one scoops water out, however, it looks quite clear in its receptacle.

Right at the very bottom there once lived a water nymph with long flowing hair. Her body was in all respects like that of a beautiful, normal woman, with one exception; between her fingers and toes she had webbing, snow-white and softer than a poppy leaf. In the little town there still stands today an old building, formerly a convent and later transformed into a large inn and consequently called The Nuns' Inn. Sixty years ago a portrait of the water nymph still hung there, its colours still distinguishable despite smoke and age. In it she had laid her hands crosswise on her breast, her countenance looked pale, her hair black, but her eyes, which were very large, blue. Amongst the people she was known as the malicious nymph in the The Blue Pool, as well as the beautiful nymph. Her behaviour towards humans was one day malicious, the next good and kind. At times, when in her ill-humour she made the pool overflow, the town and the monastery were endangered. Then the people often brought her gifts in a solemn procession, in order to appease her: gold and silver tableware, gilded goblets, bowls, little knives and other items. The monks railed against this as a heathen custom and idolatry, until it was finally stopped. Hostile as the water nymph was towards the monastery on this account, it happened not infrequently, when Father Emeran struck up the organ there and no one was about, that she half emerged from the water in broad daylight to listen. On these occasions she sometimes wore a garland of broad leaves on her head and another round her neck.

A cheeky shepherd boy was watching her one day in the bushes and cried: »Hi, tree frog! Are we going to have good weather?« Swifter than a flash of lightning and more venomously than an adder she came out, seized the boy by the hair and dragged him down into one of her watery chambers, where she would have let the by now unconscious lad languish and rot in misery. Soon, however, he came to himself again, found a door, and came up steps and through passages and many rooms to a beautiful hall. Here it was delightful and warm, even in the middle of winter. In one corner, as Lau and her maids already lay asleep, a lamp burned as a nightlight on a tall chandelier with golden bird's feet. A great deal of priceless household equipment stood around the walls, which, in addition to the stone floor, were furnished with tapestries, images woven in various colours. The boy quickly took the light down from its stand, looked round hurriedly to see what else he could lay his hands on and, from a cupboard, grabbed a bag with something extremely heavy in it, which led him to think it was gold. He then ran and came up against a little metal door, that might easily have been as thick as two fists, pushed the bolts back and climbed up a stone staircase with landings at irregular intervals, going now to the left, now to the right again. There were, to be sure, four hundred steps, which at last came to an end, and he came upon some ravines through which no paths led. Here he had to leave behind his light and so climbed for another hour back and forth in the darkness, in danger of his life, then all at once he emerged from the ground. It was dark night and he was surrounded by thick forest. When after much wandering about he finally came upon some well-worn paths with the first morning light and could see the town below from the clifftop, he felt the desire to see in daylight what was in the bag. It turned out to be nothing more than a lump of lead, a cone of a span's length, with an opening at its upper end, white with age. Angrily he threw the junk away, down into the valley, and didn't tell anybody about the theft afterwards because he was ashamed of it. Yet it was through him that the first news of the water nymph's dwelling place became public. Now the reader should know that the beautiful Lau was not a native of this place, but, as one of royal blood and indeed on her mother's side of half-human descent, was married to an old water sprite from the area where the River Danube flows into the Black Sea. Her husband banished her because she had only borne him stillborn children. The reason for her barrenness was that she was perpetually sad, without any particular reason for being so. Her mother-in-law had prophesied to her that she would not give birth to a living child until she had laughed heartily five times. On the fifth occasion this would have to happen without either her or the old sprite realising it. However, she never succeeded in her attempts, no matter how hard her servants tried to help her. Finally the old King could no longer abide her presence at his court and sent her to this place, not far from the upper Danube where his sister lived. Her mother-in-law had allowed her to take with her several chambermaids and personal maids – as cheerful and intelligent maids as ever walked on duck's feet (for all who are descended from the common line of water-sprites have proper duck's feet). They dressed her in different costumes six times a day, out of sheer boredom, for when out of the water she went about in exquis-

Zu unterst auf dem Grund saß ehmals eine Wasserfrau mit langen fließenden Haaren.

Right at the very bottom there once lived a water nymph with long flowing hair.

Im Städtlein ist noch heutzutag ein alter Bau, vormals ein Frauenkloster, hernach zu einer großen Wirtschaft eingerichtet, und hieß darum der Nonnenhof.

In the little town there still stands today an old building, formerly a convent and later transformed into a large inn and consequently called The Nuns' Inn.

So feind darum die Wasserfrau dem Kloster war, geschah es doch nicht selten, wenn Pater Emeran die Orgel drüben schlug und kein Mensch in der Nähe war, daß sie am lichten Tag mit halbem Leib heraufkam und zuhorchte; dabei trug sie zuweilen einen Kranz von breiten Blättern auf dem Kopf und auch dergleichen um den Hals.

Hostile as the water nymph was towards the monastery on this account, it happened not infrequently, when Father Emeran struck up the organ there and no one was about, that she half emerged from the water in broad daylight to listen. On these occasions she sometimes wore a garland of broad leaves on her head and another round her neck.

... und stieg eine steinerne Treppe hinauf in unterschiedlichen Absätzen, bald links, bald wieder rechts, gewiß vierhundert Stufen, bis sie zuletzt ausgingen und er auf ungeräumte Klüfte stieß ...

There were, to be sure, four hundred steps, which at last came to an end, and he came upon some ravines through which no paths led.

schichten und Mären, machten Musik, tanzten und scherzten vor ihr. An jenem Saal, darin der Hirtenbub gewesen, war der Fürstin ihr Gaden oder Schlafgemach, von welchem eine Treppe in den Blautopf ging. Da lag sie manchen lieben Tag und manche Sommernacht, der Kühluung wegen. Auch hatte sie allerlei lustige Tiere, wie Vogel, Küllhasen und Affen, vornehmlich aber einen possigen Zwerg, durch welchen vormals einem Ohm der Fürstin war von ebensolcher Traurigkeit geholfen worden. Sie spielte alle Abend Damenziehen, Schachzagel oder Schaf und Wolf mit ihm; so oft er einen ungeschickten Zug getan, schnitt er die raresten Gesichter, keines dem andern gleich, nein, immer eines ärger als das andere, daß auch der weise Salomo das Lachen nicht gehalten hatte, geschweige denn die Kammerjungfern oder du selber, liebe Leserin, wärst du dabei gewesen; nur bei der schönen Lau schlug eben gar nichts an, kaum daß sie ein paarmal den Mund verzog.

Es kamen alle Jahr um Winters Anfang Boten von daheim, die klopften an der Halle mit dem Hammer, da frugen dann die Jungfern:

»Wer pochet, daß einem das Herz erschrickt?«

Und jene sprachen:

»Der König schickt!
Gebt uns wahrhaftigen Bescheid,
Was Guts ihr habt geschafft die Zeit.«

Und sie sagten:

»Wir haben die ferndigen Lieder gesungen,
Und haben die ferndigen Tänze gesprungen,
Gewonnen war es um ein Haar! –
Kommt, liebe Herren, übers Jahr.«

So zogen sie wieder nach Haus. Die Frau war aber vor der Botschaft und darnach stets noch einmal so traurig.

Im Nonnenhof war eine dicke Wirtin, Frau Betha Seysolffin, ein frohes Biederweib, christlich, leutselig, gütig; zumal an armen reisenden Gesellen bewies sie sich als eine rechte Fremdenmutter. Die Wirtschaft führte zumeist ihr ältester Sohn, Stephan, welcher verehlicht war; ein anderer, Xaver, war Klosterkoch, zwo Töchter noch bei ihr. Sie hatte einen kleinen Küchengarten vor der Stadt, dem Topf zunächst. Als sie im Frühjahr einst am ersten warmen Tag dort war und ihre Beete richtete, den Kappis, den Salat zu säen, Bohnen und Zwiebel zu stecken, besah sie sich von ungefähr auch einmal recht mit Wohlgefallen wieder das schöne blaue Wasser überm Zaun und mit Verdruß daneben einen alten garstigen Schutthügel, der schändete den ganzen Platz; nahm also, wie sie fertig war mit ihrer Arbeit und das Gartentürlein hinter sich zugemacht hatte, die Hacke noch einmal, riß flink das gröbste Unkraut aus, erlas etliche Kürbiskern' aus ihrem Samenkorb und steckte hin und wieder einen in den Haufen. (Der Abt im Kloster, der die Wirtin, als eine saubere Frau, gern sah – man hatte sie nicht über vierzig Jahr geschätzt, er selber aber war gleich ihr ein starkbeleibter Herr – stand just am Fenster oben und grüßte herüber, indem er mit dem Finger drohte, als halte sie zu seiner Widersacherin.) Die Wüstung grünte nun den ganzen Sommer, daß es eine Freude war, und hingen dann im Herbst die großen gelben Kürbis an dem Abhang nieder bis zu dem Teich.

Jetzt ging einsmals der Wirtin Tochter, Jutta, in den Keller, woselbst sich noch von alten Zeiten her ein offener Brunnen mit einem steinernen Kasten befand. Beim Schein des Lichts erblickte sie darinne mit Entsetzen die schöne Lau, schwebend bis an die Brust im Wasser; sprang voller Angst davon und sagts der Mutter an; die fürchtete sich nicht und stieg allein hinunter, litt auch nicht, daß ihr der Sohn zum Schutz nachfolge, weil das Weib nackt war.

Der wunderliche Gast sprach diesen Gruß:

»Die Wasserfrau ist kommen
Gekrochen und geschwommen,
Durch Gange steinig, wüst und kraus,
Zur Wirtin in das Nonnenhaus.
Sie hat sich meinethalb gebückt,
Mein Topf geschmückt
Mit Früchten und mit Ranken,
Das muß ich billig danken.«

Sie hatte einen Kreisel aus wasserhellem Stein in ihrer Hand, den gab sie der Wirtin und sagte: »Nehmt dieses Spielzeug, liebe Frau, zu meinem Angedenken. Ihr werdet guten Nutzen davon haben. Denn jüngsthin habe ich gehört, wie Ihr in Eurem Garten der Nachbarin klagtet, Euch sei schon auf die Kirchweih angst, wo immer die Bürger und Bauern zu Unfrieden kämen und Mord und Totschlag zu befahren sei. Derhalben, liebe Frau, wenn wieder die trunkenen Gäste bei Tanz und Zeche Streit beginnen, nehmt den Topf zur Hand und dreht ihn vor der Tür des Saals im Öhrn, da wird man hören durch das ganze Haus ein mächtiges und herrliches Getöne, daß alle gleich die Fäuste werden sinken lassen und guter Dinge sein, denn jählings ist ein jeder nüchtern und gescheit geworden. Ist es an dem, so werfet Eure Schürze auf den Topf, da wickelt er sich alsbald ein und lieget stille.«

So redete das Wasserweib. Frau Betha nahm vergnügt das Kleinod samt der goldenen Schnur und dem Halter von Ebenholz, rief ihrer Tochter

ite garments, although barefoot. They related old stories and tales to her, made music, and danced and jested in her presence. In the hall where the young shepherd had been was the princess's bedchamber, from which a staircase led up to the Blue Pool. On many a nice day and summer's night she lay there to keep cool. She also had all kinds of amusing animals – birds, rabbits and monkeys, and in particular a comical dwarf, through whom an uncle of hers had been helped to overcome a similar sadness. Every evening she played draughts, chess, or a board game called sheep and wolf with him. Each time he made a careless move he pulled the most terrible faces, each one different from the other, each one worse than the other, so that even Solomon the Wise could not have helped laughing, let alone the chambermaids, or you yourself, dear reader, if you had been there. But nothing had any effect on the beautiful Lau – indeed she barely did more than contort her lips a few times.

Every year at the beginning of winter, messengers came from home who hammered at the hall door, so that the maidens asked:

»Who knocks, to startle us in our hearts?«

And they answered:

»The king sends us!
Tell us truly what good things
you have done since our last visit.«

And the maidens said:

»We have sung last year's songs,
and have tripped last year's dances.
We came very close to success!
Come again, dear sirs, in a year's time.«

So they returned home again. But Lau was still just as sad after their visit as she had been before.

In the Nuns' Inn there was a rather fat landlady, Mrs Betha Seysolff, a cheerful, honest woman, a good Christian, genial and kind. She was a proper second mother to poor travelling journeymen. The inn was run mostly by her eldest son, Stephan, a married man. Another son, Xaver, was the monastery cook, and two daughters were still at home. She had a little vegetable garden outside the town, by the Blue Pool. When she was once there on the first warm day of spring, preparing the ground, sowing cabbage and lettuce seeds and planting out beans and onions, she happened to see, with much pleasure, the lovely blue water on the other side of the hedge, and, with a good deal of frustration a horrible pile of rubble next to it, which spoilt the whole area. So when she had completed her work and closed the little garden gate behind her, she took up her hoe once again and deftly pulled out the worst of the weeds, selected a few pumpkin seeds from her seed basket and planted one here and there on the mound. (The abbot in the monastery, who liked to see the landlady whom he regarded as a handsome woman – one would not have taken her to be over forty years old and he himself was, like her, a fairly corpulent person – was just standing at a window and waved to her, raising his finger threateningly, as if she were in league with his adversary, Lau.) Now the neglected patch blossomed all summer, so that it was a joy to behold, and then in the autumn the big yellow pumpkins hung down the slope as far as the pond.

One day the landlady's daughter, Jutta, went down to the cellar where from time immemorial there had been an open well with a stone basin. In the glow of the lamp she could see, to her horror, the beautiful Lau just emerging from the water. Full of anxiety she rushed away to tell her mother what she had seen. The latter was not at all afraid and went down alone, nor would she allow her son to follow her to protect her, because the woman was naked.

The strange guest greeted her thus:

»The water nymph has come
Crawling and swimming,
Through stony passages, desolate and crooked,
To the landlady of the Nuns' Inn.
For my sake she bent her back
To adorn my little lake
With fruits and tendrils,
For which I thank her heartily.«

In her hand the nymph had a humming-top made of transparent stone which she gave to the landlady saying: »Take this toy, dear lady, in remembrance of me. It will be very useful to you. Recently I heard you complaining in your garden to your neighbour that you are already anxious about the fair when the locals always end up fighting, and murder and manslaughter are to be feared. So, dear lady, the next time your drunken guests start righting while dancing and drinking, pick up the top and spin it outside the door in the hall. Then a powerful but beautiful resonant sound will be heard throughout the house, so that they will all lower their fists and be in good spirits, for they will all immediately become sensible and sober. When this happens throw down your apron and it will immediately wrap itself round the top and bring it to a stand still.«

So said the water nymph. With much pleasure Mrs Betha accepted this precious gift, together

Die Schwiegermutter hatte ihr zum Dienst und Zeitvertreib etliche Kammerzofen und Mägde mitgegeben, so muntere und kluge Mädchen, als je auf Entenfüßen gingen (denn was von dem gemeinen Stamm der Wasserweiber ist, hat rechte Entenfüße); die zogen sie, pur für die Langeweile, sechsmal des Tages anders an ...

Her mother-in-law had allowed her to take with her several chambermaids and personal maids – as cheerful and intelligent maids as ever walked on duck's feet (for all who are descended from the common line of water-sprites have proper duck's feet). They dressed her in different costumes six times a day ...

An jenem Saal, darin der Hirtenbub gewesen, war der Fürstin ihr Gaden oder Schlafgemach, von welchem eine Treppe in den Blautopf ging. Da lag sie manchen lieben Tag und manche Sommernacht, der Kühlung wegen.

In the hall where the young shepherd had been was the princess's bedchamber, from which a staircase led up to the Blue Pool. On many a nice day and summer's night she lay there to keep cool.

Die Wasserfrau kam jeden Mond einmal, auch je und je unverhofft zwischen der Zeit, weshalb die Wirtin eine Schelle richten ließ, oben im Haus, mit einem Draht, der lief herunter an der Wand beim Brunnen, damit sie sich gleichbald anzeigen konnte.

The water nymph came once every month and occasionally quite unexpectedly in the meantime, so that the landlady had a bell installed upstairs in the house, with a wire running down the wall by the well for the nymph to announce her presence.

»Derhalben, liebe Frau, wenn wieder die trunkenen Gäste bei Tanz und Zeche Streit beginnen, nehmt den Topf zur Hand und dreht ihn vor der Tür des Saals im Öhrn, da wird man hören durch das ganze Haus ein mächtiges und herrliches Getöne, daß alle gleich die Fäuste werden sinken lassen und guter Dinge sein ...«

»So, dear lady, the next time your drunken guests start righting while dancing and drinking, pick up the top and spin it outside the door in the hall. Then a powerful but beautiful resonant sound will be heard throughout the house, so that they will all lower their fists and be in good spirits, for they will all immediately become sensible and sober ...«

Im Nonnenhof war eine dicke Wirtin, Frau Betha Seysolffin, ein frohes Biederweib, christlich, leutselig, gütig; zumal an armen reisenden Gesellen bewies sie sich als eine rechte Fremdenmutter.

In the Nuns' Inn there was a rather fat landlady, Mrs Betha Seysolff, a cheerful, honest woman, a good Christian, genial and kind.

Jutta her (sie stand nur hinter dem Krautfaß an der Staffel), wies ihr die Gabe, dankte und lud die Frau, so oft die Zeit ihr lang war, freundlich ein zu fernerem Besuch; darauf das Weib hinabfuhr und verschwand.

Es dauerte nicht lang, so wurde offenbar, welch einen Schatz die Wirtschaft an dem Topf gewann. Denn nicht allein, daß er durch seine Kraft und hohe Tugend die übeln Händel allezeit in einer Kurze dämpfte, er brachte auch dem Gasthaus bald erstaunliche Einkehr zuwege. Wer in die Gegend kam, gemein oder vornehm, ging ihm zulieb; insonderheit kam bald der Graf von Helfenstein, von Wirtemberg und etliche große Prälaten; ja ein berühmter Herzog aus Lombardenland, so bei dem Herzoge von Bayern gastweis war und dieses Wegs nach Frankreich reiste, bot vieles Geld für dieses Stück, wenn es die Wirtin lassen wollte. Gewiß auch war in keinem andern Land seinesgleichen zu sehn und zu hören. Erst, wenn er anhub sich zu drehen, ging es doucement her, dann klang es stärker und stärker, so hoch wie tief, und immer herrlicher, als wie der Schall von vielen Pfeifen, der quoll und stieg durch alle Stockwerke bis unter das Dach und bis in den Keller, dergestalt, daß alle Wände, Dielen, Säulen und Geländer schienen davon erfüllt zu sein, zu tönen und zu schwellen. Wenn nun das Tuch auf ihn geworfen wurde und er ohnmächtig lag, so hörte gleichwohl die Musik sobald nicht auf, es zog vielmehr der ausgeladene Schwall mit starkem Klingen, Dröhnen, Summen noch wohl bei einer Viertelstunde hin und her.

Bei uns im Schwabenland heißt so ein Topf aus Holz gemeinhin eine Habergeis; Frau Betha ihrer ward nach seinem vornehmsten Geschäfte insgemein genannt der Bauren-Schwaiger. Er war gemacht aus einem großen Amethyst, dess' Name besagen will: wider den Trunk; weil er den schweren Dunst des Weins geschwinde aus dem Kopf vertreibt, ja schon von Anbeginn dawider tut, daß einen guten Zecher das Selige berühre; darum ihn auch weltlich und geistliche Herren sonst häufig pflegten am Finger zu tragen.

Die Wasserfrau kam jeden Mond einmal, auch je und je unverhofft zwischen der Zeit, weshalb die Wirtin eine Schelle richten ließ, oben im Haus, mit einem Draht, der lief herunter an der Wand beim Brunnen, damit sie sich gleichbald anzeigen konnte. Also ward sie je mehr und mehr zutunlich zu den wackeren Frauen, der Mutter samt den Töchtern und der Söhnerin.

Einsmals an einem Nachmittag im Sommer, da eben keine Gäste kamen, der Sohn mit den Knechten und Mägden hinaus in das Heu gefahren war, Frau Betha mit der Ältesten im Keller Wein abließ, die Lau im Brunnen aber Kurzweil halben dem Geschäft zusah und nun die Frauen noch ein wenig mit ihr plauderten: da fing die Wirtin an: »Mögt Ihr Euch denn einmal in meinem Haus und Hof umsehn? Die Jutta konnte Euch etwas von Kleidern geben; ihr seid von einer Größe.«

»Ja«, sagte sie, »ich wollte lange gern die Wohnungen der Menschen sehn, was alles sie darin gewerben, spinnen, weben, ingleichen auch wie Eure Töchter Hochzeit machen und ihre kleinen Kinder in der Wiege schwenken.«

Da lief die Tochter fröhlich mit Eile hinauf, ein rein Leintuch zu holen, bracht es und half ihr aus dem Kasten steigen, das tat sie sonder Mühe und lachenden Mundes. Flugs schlug ihr die Dirne das Tuch um den Leib und führte sie bei ihrer Hand eine schmale Stiege hinauf in der hintersten Ecke des Kellers, da man durch eine Falltür oben gleich in der Tochter Kammer gelangt. Allda ließ sie sich trocken machen und saß auf einem Stuhl, indem ihr Jutta die Füße abrieb. Wie diese ihr nun an die Sohle kam, fuhr sie zurück und kicherte.

»Wars nicht gelacht?« frug sie selber sogleich. – »Was anders?« rief das Mädchen und jauchzte; »gebenedeiet sei uns der Tag! ein erstes Mal war es geglückt!« – Die Wirtin hörte in der Küche das Gelächter und die Freude, kam herein, begierig, wie es zugegangen, doch als sie die Ursach vernommen – du armer Tropf, so dachte sie, das wird ja schwerlich gelten! – ließ sich indes nichts merken, und Jutta nahm etliche Stücke heraus aus dem Schrank, das Beste, was sie hatte, die Hausfreundin zu kleiden. »Seht«, sagte die Mutter, »sie will wohl aus Euch eine Susann Preisnestel machen.« – »Nein«, rief die Lau in ihrer Fröhlichkeit; »laß mich die Aschengruttel sein in deinem Märchen!« – nahm einen schlechten runden Faltenrock und eine Jacke; nicht Schuh noch Strümpfe litt sie an den Füßen, auch hingen ihre Haare ungezöpft bis auf die Knöchel nieder. So strich sie durch das Haus von unten bis zu oberst, durch Küche, Stuben und Gemächer. Sie verwunderte sich des gemeinsten Gerätes und seines Gebrauchs, besah den rein gefegten Schenktisch und darüber in langen Reihen die zinnenen Kannen und Gläser, alle gleich gestürzt, mit hängendem Deckel, dazu den kupfernen Schwenkkessel samt der Bürste, und mitten in der Stube an der Decke der Weber Zunftgeschmuck, mit Seidenband und Silberdraht geziert, in dem Kästlein von Glas. Von ungefähr erblickte sie ihr eigen Bild im Spiegel, davor blieb sie betroffen und erstockt eine ganze Weile stehn, und als darauf die Söhnerin sie mit in ihre Stube nahm und ihr ein neues Spiegelein, drei Groschen wert, verehrte, da meinte sie Wunders zu haben, denn unter allen ihren Schätzen fand sich dergleichen nicht.

Bevor sie aber Abschied nahm, geschahs, daß sie hinter den Vorhang des Alkoven schaute,

with its golden cord and ebony box. She called her daughter Jutta over (she was standing just behind the barrel of pickled cabbage by the stone steps) and showed her the gift. She thanked the nymph and invited her to visit them again whenever time hung heavy. Thereupon the nymph descended into the depths again and disappeared. It didn't take long to become obvious what a treasure the inn had acquired in the top. Not only did it through its power and great virtue subdue the unpleasant squabbles whenever they occurred, but it also brought an astonishing number of guests to the inn. Whoever came into the area, whether high or low born, came simply because of the inn; in particular came the Counts von Helfenstein and von Wirtemberg, as well as a number of important prelates. Indeed, a famous duke from Lombardy, who had been a guest of the Duke of Bavaria and was travelling by this route to France offered a great deal of money for this item, if the landlady was prepared to sell it. Certainly its like was not to be seen or heard of in any other country. When it first began to spin there was a sweet sound, which then became louder and louder, with both a high and a low note. This welled up and penetrated into all the storeys, both up into the roof and down into the cellar, to such an extent that all the walls, hallways, pillars and bannisters seemed to be filled by it, to echo and to swell. When a cloth was thrown over the top and it lay still, the music did not cease at once, but rather the dying flood of sound moved back and forth for perhaps a quarter of an hour with a loud ringing, booming and humming.

Here in Swabia a wooden top of this type is generally known as a Habergeis, which is our dialect name for a humming top. Because of its very important effect Mrs Betha's was usually called the Peasant Silencer. It was made of a large amethyst, the name of which implies: against drink, because it quickly drives the heavy haze of wine from the head, and even from the very beginning prevents a drinker from reaching a state of blessedness; for this reason both secular and clerical gentlemen in former times frequently wore an amethyst ring on their finger.

The water nymph came once every month and occasionally quite unexpectedly in the meantime, so that the landlady had a bell installed upstairs in the house, with a wire running down the wall by the well for the nymph to announce her presence. In this way she became more and more trusting toward the honest ladies, i.e. the mother, as well as her daughters and daughter-in-law. One summer afternoon, as no guests happened to be arriving, the son, together with the servants, both male and female, had gone haymaking. Mrs Betha with her eldest daughter was decanting wine in the cellar, and Lau, to pass the time away, watched their activity from the well. The women chatted with her for a while, then Mrs Betha said: »Would you like to look around my house some time? Jutta could give you some clothes; you are about the same size.«

»Yes«, she said, »I have long since wanted to see the dwellings of human beings, the work they do in them, how they spin and weave, and also the way in which your daughters marry and rock their little children in their cradles.«

Thereupon the daughter rushed happily upstairs to fetch a clean sheet, brought it down and helped her to climb out of the well, which she did without any bother and with a smile on her lips. Without delay the girl threw the sheet around Lau's body and led her by the hand up a narrow staircase in the very rear corner of the cellar, as one could get directly into the daughters' room through a trapdoor at the top. There the nymph let herself be dried, sitting on a chair while Jutta wiped her feet. When the latter dried the sole of her foot she jerked back and giggled. »Didn't I laugh then?« she immediately asked. »What else?« exclaimed the girl joyfully. »Blessed be the day! Success for the first time!« The landlady in the kitchen heard the laughter and the joy and came in, eager to know what had been going on, but when she heard the reason she thought: »You poor thing! That will hardly have any effect!« However she didn't show her feelings. Jutta took a few things out of her cupboard, the best that she had, to dress her friend in. »Look«, said her mother, »she wants to make a Susann Preisnestel of you.« »No«, exclaimed Lau in her happy mood, »let me be Cinderella in your fairy tale« – and she took a shabby pleated skirt and a jacket. She would not allow shoes or stockings to be put on her feet, and her unplatted hair hung down to her ankles. Thus she wandered through the house from top to bottom, through kitchen, living rooms and chambers. She was amazed at the most common implements and their uses, and inspected the cleanly swept bar and above it, in long rows, the pewter tankards and glasses, all turned upside down with their lids hanging open. She also saw the hanging copper cauldron with its brush, and in the middle of the room, on the ceiling, the coat of arms of the guild of weavers, decorated with silk ribbon and silver wire, in its little glass casket. By chance she caught sight of her own image in the mirror and stood before it for a while, amazed and taken aback, and when the daughter-in-law later took her to her room and gave her a new little mirror, worth a few coppers, she thought she had something magic. Amongst all her treasures she had nothing like this.

Allda ließ sie sich trocken machen und saß auf einem Stuhl, indem ihr Jutta die Füße abrieb. Wie diese ihr nun an die Sohle kam, fuhr sie zurück und kicherte.

There the nymph let herself be dried, sitting on a chair while Jutta wiped her feet. When the latter dried the sole of her foot she jerked back and giggled.

»Nein«, rief die Lau in ihrer Fröhlichkeit; »laß mich die Aschengruttel sein in deinem Märchen« – *nahm einen schlechten runden Faltenrock und eine Jacke; nicht Schuh noch Strümpfe litt sie an den Füßen, auch hingen ihre Haare ungezöpft bis auf die Knöchel nieder.*

»No«, exclaimed Lau in her happy mood, »let me be Cinderella in your fairy tale« – and she took a shabby pleated skirt and a jacket. She would not allow shoes or stockings to be put on her feet, and her unplatted hair hung down to her ankles.

woselbst der jungen Frau und ihres Mannes Bett sowie der Kinder Schlafstätte war. Saß da ein Enkelein mit rotgeschlafenen Backen, hemdig und einen Apfel in der Hand, auf einem runden Stühlchen von guter Ulmer Hafnerarbeit, grünverglaset. Das wollte dem Gast außer Maßen gefallen; sie nannte es einen viel zierlichen Sitz, rümpft' aber die Nase mit eins, und da die drei Frauen sich wandten zu lachen, vermerkte sie etwas und fing auch hell zu lachen an, und hielt sich die ehrliche Wirtin den Bauch, indem sie sprach: »Diesmal fürwahr hat es gegolten, und Gott schenk Euch so einen frischen Buben, als mein Hans da ist!«

Die Nacht darauf, daß sich dies zugetragen, legte sich die schöne Lau getrost und wohlgemut, wie schon in langen Jahren nicht, im Grund des Blautopfs nieder, schlief gleich ein, und bald erschien ihr ein närrischer Traum.

Ihr deuchte da, es war die Stunde nach Mittag, wo in der heißen Jahreszeit die Leute auf der Wiese sind und mähen, die Mönche aber sich in ihren kühlen Zellen eine Ruhe machen, daher es noch einmal so still im ganzen Kloster und rings um seine Mauern war. Es stund jedoch nicht lange an, so kam der Abt herausspaziert und sah, ob nicht etwa die Wirtin in ihrem Garten sei. Dieselbe aber saß als eine dicke Wasserfrau mit langen Haaren in dem Topf, allwo der Abt sie bald entdeckte, sie begrüßte und ihr einen Kuß gab, so mächtig, daß es vom Klostertürmlein widerschallte, und schallte es der Turm ans Refektorium, das sagt' es der Kirche und die sagt's dem Pferdstall und der sagt's dem Fischhaus und das sagt's dem Waschhaus und im Waschhaus da riefen's die Zuber und Kübel sich zu. Der Abt erschrak bei solchem Lärm; ihm war, wie er sich nach der Wirtin blickte, sein Käpplein in Blautopf gefallen, sie gab es ihm geschwind, und er watschelte hurtig davon.

Da aber kam aus dem Kloster heraus unser Herrgott, zu sehn, was es gebe. Er hatte einen langen weißen Bart und einen roten Rock. Und frug den Abt, der ihm just in die Hände lief:

»Herr Abt, wie ward Euer Käpplein so naß?«

Und er antwortete:

»Es ist mir ein Wildschwein am Wald verkommen,
Vor dem hab ich Reißaus genommen;
Ich rannte sehr und schwitzet' baß,
Davon ward wohl mein Käpplein so naß.«

Da hob unser Herrgott, unwiß ob der Lüge, seinen Finger auf, winkt' ihm und ging voran, dem Kloster zu. Der Abt sah hehlings noch einmal nach der Frau Wirtin um, und diese rief:

»Ach liebe Zeit, ach liebe Zeit, jetzt kommt der gut' alt' Herr in die Prison!«

Dies war der schönen Lau ihr Traum. Sie wußte aber beim Erwachen und spürte noch an ihrem Herzen, daß sie im Schlaf sehr lachte, und ihr hüpfte noch wachend die Brust, daß der Blautopf oben Ringlein schlug.

Weil es den Tag zuvor sehr schwül gewesen, so blitzte es jetzt in der Nacht. Der Schein erhellte den Blautopf ganz, auch spürte sie am Boden, es donnere weitweg. So blieb sie mit zufriedenem Gemüte noch eine Weile ruhen, den Kopf in ihre Hand gestützt, und sah dem Wetterblicken zu. Nun stieg sie auf, zu wissen, ob der Morgen etwa komme: allein es war noch nicht viel über Mitternacht. Der Mond stand glatt und schön über dem Rusenschloß, die Lüfte aber waren voll vom Würzgeruch der Mahden.

Sie meinte fast der Geduld nicht zu haben bis an die Stunde, wo sie im Nonnenhof ihr neues Glück verkünden durfte, ja wenig fehlte, daß sie sich jetzt nicht mitten in der Nacht aufmachte und vor Juttas Türe kam (wie sie nur einmal, Trostes wegen, in übergroßem Jammer nach der jüngsten Botschaft aus der Heimat, tat), doch sie besann sich anders und ging zu besserer Zeit. Frau Betha hörte ihren Traum gutmütig an, obwohl er ihr ein wenig ehrenrührig schien. Bedenklich aber sagte sie darauf: »Baut nicht auf solches Lachen, das im Schlaf geschah; der Teufel ist ein Schelm. Wenn Ihr auf solches Trugwerk hin die Boten mit fröhlicher Zeitung entließet, und die Zukunft strafte Euch Lügen, es könnte schlimm daheim ergehen.«

Auf diese ihre Rede hing die schöne Lau den Mund gar sehr und sagte: »Frau Ahne hat der Traum verdrossen!« – nahm kleinlauten Abschied und tauchte hinunter.

Es war nah bei Mittag, da rief der Pater Schaffner im Kloster dem Bruder Kellermeister eifrig zu: »Ich merk, es ist im Gumpen letz! Die Arge will Euch Eure Faß wohl wieder einmal schwimmen lehren. Tut Eure Läden eilig zu, vermachet alles wohl!«

Nun aber war des Klosters Koch, der Wirtin Sohn, ein lustiger Vogel, welchen die Lau wohl leiden mochte. Der dachte ihren Jäst mit einem Schnak zu stillen, lief nach seiner Kammer, zog die Bettscher aus der Lagerstätte und steckte sie am Blautopf in den Rasen, wo das Wasser auszutreten pflegte, und stellte sich mit Worten und Gebärden als einen viel getreuen Diener an, der mächtig Ängsten hatte, daß seine Herrschaft aus dem Bette fallen und etwa Schaden nehmen möchte. Da sie nun sah das Holz so recht mit Fleiß gesteckt und über das Bächlein gespreizt, kam ihr in ihrem Zorn das Lachen an, und lachte überlaut, daß man's im Klostergarten hörte.

Before she left, she happened to peep behind the curtain of the alcove where the young woman's and her husband's bed was, as well as the children's sleeping area. A little grandchild, its cheeks still red from sleep, in its little vest and with an apple in its hand, was sitting there on a little round chamber pot made of good Ulm pottery and glazed green. This amused the guest beyond measure. She said it was a very dainty seat, but all at once turned up her nose, and when the three women turned away to laugh, something took her notice and she also began to laugh heartily, so that the good landlady held her stomach saying: »This time it's worked, and may God present you with such a bright lad as my Hans is!«

On the night after this had happened, the lovely Lau lay down in the depths of the Blue Pool more reassured and cheerful than she had been for many long years. She immediately fell asleep and was soon in the midst of a crazy dream.

It seemed to her that it was the hour after noon when in high summer the people are in the meadow cutting grass, but the monks take a rest in the cool cells so that it was once again so quiet in the whole monastery and around its walls. It was not long however before the abbot came out to see whether the landlady was perhaps in her garden. She was sitting like a fat water nymph with long hair in the pool, where the abbot soon discovered her, greeted her, and gave her such a tremendous kiss that it echoed from the monastery tower. It resounded from the tower to the refectory, the latter passed it on to the church, which told the stable, the stable told the fish house, the fish house told the laundry, and in the laundry it resounded from the washtubs to the buckets. The abbot was alarmed at such a noise. As he bent down towards the landlady his calotte had fallen into the Blue Pool. She hastily handed it to him and he waddled hurriedly away.

But then our Lord God came out of the monastery to see what was going on. He had a long white beard and was wearing a red coat. He asked the abbot, who at that moment came face to face with him:

»Lord Abbot, how did your cap get so wet?«

and he answered:

»A wild boar came charging at me in the forest,
And I had to take to my heels.
I ran so quickly and sweated so much,
And that I suppose is how my cap got so wet.«

Thereupon our Lord God, annoyed by the lie, wagged his finger at him and went away towards the monastery. The abbot looked round furtively again at the landlady, and she cried: »Oh dear, oh dear, now the good old gentleman will go to prison.«

That was the beautiful Lau's dream. She knew though on awakening and could still feel it in her heart that she had laughed in her sleep, and her bosom was still swelling so much for joy, that there were ripples on the surface of the Blue Pool.

Because the previous day had been very sultry, there was a thunderstorm during the night. The lightning lit up the entire Blue Pool and down in the depths she sensed thunder in the distance. So she remained lying down for a while, her head in her hand in a contented frame of mind, watching the lightning. Then she got up to see whether morning was approaching, but it was not yet much past midnight. The moon stood clear and beautiful over the Rusen castle, and the breezes were fall of the fragrant smell of mown grass.

She thought she would hardly have sufficient patience to wait for the hour when she could announce her new happiness at The Nuns' Inn. It wouldn't have needed much to make her get up now in the middle of the night, and make her way to Jutta's door, (something she had done only once, seeking consolation in her extreme misery at the latest news from home), but she thought better of it and went at a more convenient time. Mrs Betha listened to her dream good-humouredly, although it seemed to her somewhat slanderous. Thoughtfully she said:

»Don't build your hopes on such laughter that occurs in your sleep. The devil is a mischiefmaker. If you dismissed the messengers with cheerful news as a result of this deception, and the future proved you wrong, things could go badly for you at home.«

At these words Lau was very down in the mouth and said: »The dream annoyed you, I can see.« She meekly took her leave and immersed herself in the water.

It was almost noon when the friar administrator of the monastery called to the cellarer: »I see there's something amiss in the pool! The wicked nymph no doubt wants to teach your barrels to swim again. Hurry up and close your shutters and make everything safe.«

However the monastery cook, the landlady's son, was a lively character of whom Lau was quite fond. He thought he would overcome her annoyance with a joke, and he ran to his room, fetched the bed-guard from the bed and stuck it in the grass by the Blue Pool where the water usually came out. There, with words and gestures, he acted like a very loyal servant who greatly feared that his master might fall out of

Saß da ein Enkelein mit rotgeschlafenen Backen, hemdig und einen Apfel in der Hand, auf einem runden Stühlchen von guter Ulmer Hafnerarbeit, grünverglaset.

A little grandchild, its cheeks still red from sleep, in its little vest and with an apple in its hand, was sitting there on a little round chamber pot made of good Ulm pottery and glazed green.

Der Mond stand glatt und schön über dem Rusenschloß, die Lüfte aber waren voll vom Würzgeruch der Mahden.

The moon stood clear and beautiful over the Rusen castle, and the breezes were fall of the fragrant smell of mown grass.

Als sie hierauf am Abend zu den Frauen kam, da wußten sie es schon vom Koch und wünschten ihr mit tausend Freuden Glück. Die Wirtin sagte: »der Xaver ist von Kindesbeinen an gewesen als wie der Zauberclaus, jetzt kommt uns seine Torheit zustatten.«

Nun aber ging ein Monat nach dem andern herum, es wollte sich zum dritten- oder viertenmal nicht wieder schicken. Martini war vorbei, noch wenig Wochen, und die Boten standen wieder vor der Tür. Da ward es den guten Wirtsleuten selbst bang, ob heuer noch etwas zustande käme, und alle hatten nur zu trösten an der Frau. Je größer deren Angst, je weniger zu hoffen war.

Damit sie ihres Kummers eher vergesse, lud ihr Frau Betha einen Lichtkarz ein, da nach dem Abendessen ein halb Dutzend muntre Dirnen und Weiber aus der Verwandtschaft in einer abgelegenen Stube mit ihren Kunkeln sich zusammensetzten. Die Lau kam alle Abend in Juttas altem Rock und Kittel und ließ sich weit vom warmen Ofen weg in einem Winkel auf den Boden nieder und hörte dem Geplauder zu, von Anfang als ein stummer Gast, ward aber bald zutraulich und bekannt mit allen. Um ihretwillen machte sich Frau Betha eines Abends ein Geschäft daraus, ihr Weihnachtskripplein für die Enkel beizeiten herzurichten: die Mutter Gottes mit dem Kind im Stall, bei ihr die drei Weisen aus Morgenland, ein jeder mit seinem Kamel, darauf er hergereist kam und seine Gaben brachte. Dies alles aufzuputzen und zu leimen, was etwa lotter war, saß die Frau Wirtin an dem Tisch beim Licht mit ihrer Brille, und die Wasserfrau mit höchlichem Ergötzen sah ihr zu, sowie sie auch gerne vernahm, was ihr von heiligen Geschichten dabei gesagt wurde, doch nicht, daß sie dieselben dem rechten Verstand nach begriff oder zu Herzen nahm, wie gern auch die Wirtin es wollte.

Frau Betha wußte ferner viel lehrreicher Fabeln und Denkreime, auch spitzweise Fragen und Rätsel; die gab sie nacheinander im Vorsitz aufzuraten, weil sonderlich die Wasserfrau von Hause aus dergleichen liebte und immer gar zufrieden schien, wenn sie es ein und das andre Mal traf (das doch nicht allzu leicht geriet). Eines derselben gefiel ihr vor allen, und was damit gemeint ist, nannte sie ohne Besinnen:

»Ich bin eine dürre Königin,
Trag auf dem Haupt eine zierliche Kron,
Und die mir dienen mit treuem Sinn,
Die haben großen Lohn.

Meine Frauen müssen mich schon frisieren,
Erzählen mir Märlein ohne Zahl,
Sie lassen kein einzig Haar an mir,
Doch siehst du mich nimmer kahl.

Spazieren fahr ich frank und frei,
Das geht so rasch, das geht so fein;
Nur komm ich nicht vom Platz dabei –
Sagt, Leute, was mag das sein?«

Darüber sagte sie, in etwas fröhlicher denn zuvor: »Wenn ich dereinstens wiederum in meiner Heimat bin, und kommt einmal ein schwäbisch Landeskind, zumal aus eurer Stadt, auf einer Kriegsfahrt oder sonst durch der Walachen Land an unsere Gestade, so ruf er mich bei Namen, dort wo der Strom am breitesten hineingeht in das Meer – versteht, zehn Meilen einwärts in dieselbe See erstreckt sich meines Mannes Reich, soweit das süße Wasser sie mit seiner Farbe färbt –, dann will ich kommen und dem Fremdling zu Rat und Hilfe sein. Damit er aber sicher sei, ob ich es bin und keine andere, die ihm schaden möchte, so stelle er dies Rätsel. Niemand aus unserem Geschlechte außer mir wird ihm darauf antworten; denn dortzuland sind solche Rocken und Rädlein, als ihr in Schwaben führt, nicht gesehn, noch kennen sie dort eure Sprache; darum mag dies die Losung sein.«

Auf einen andern Abend ward erzählt vom Doktor Veylland und Herrn Conrad von Wirtemberg, dem alten Gaugrafen, in dessen Tagen es noch keine Stadt mit Namen Stuttgart gab. Im Wiesental, da wo dieselbe sich nachmals erhob, stund nur ein stattliches Schloß mit Wassergraben und Zugbrücke; von Bruno, dem Domherrn von Speyer, Conradens Oheim, erbaut, und nicht gar weit davon ein hohes steinernes Haus. In diesem wohnte dazumal mit einem alten Diener ganz allein ein sonderlicher Mann, der war in natürlicher Kunst und in Arzneikunst sehr gelehrt und war mit seinem Herrn, dem Grafen, weit in der Welt herumgereist, in heißen Ländern, von wo er manche Seltsamkeit an Tieren, vielerlei Gewächsen und Meerwundern heraus nach Schwaben brachte. In seinem Ohr sah man der fremden Sachen eine Menge an den Wänden herum hangen: die Haut vom Krokodil sowie Schlangen und fliegende Fische. Fast alle Wochen kam der Graf einmal zu ihm; mit andern Leuten pflegte er wenig Gemeinschaft. Man wollte behaupten, er mache Gold; gewiß ist, daß er sich unsichtbar machen konnte, denn er verwahrte unter seinem Kram einen Krackenfischzahn. Einst nämlich, als er auf dem Roten Meer das Bleilot niederließ, die Tiefe zu erforschen, da zockt' es unterm Wasser, daß das Tau fast riß. Es hatte sich ein Krackenfisch im Lot verbissen und zween seiner Zähne darinne gelassen. Sie sind wie eine Schustersahle spitz und glänzend schwarz. Der eine stak sehr fest, der andre ließ sich leicht ausziehen. Da nun ein solcher Zahn, etwa in Silber oder Gold gefaßt und bei sich getragen, besagte hohe Kraft besitzt und zu den

bed and be injured. When she now saw the wooden structure positioned so carefully and spread across the little stream, she started to laugh even in her anger, and indeed so loudly that she could be heard in the monastery garden. When she visited the women later in the evening, they already knew all about the incident from the cook and congratulated her with great joy. The landlady said: »Xaver has always been from childhood a bit of a clown. Now his nonsense has come in useful for us.«

Now one month went by after another without her succeeding in laughing a third or fourth time. St. Martin's Day was past, and in a few more weeks her husband's messengers were at the door again. Even the good people of the inn were afraid that nothing comparable would happen this year either, and there was nothing they could all do except console her. The greater her anxiety, the less there was to hope for.

In order that she might forget her sorrows more quickly, Mrs Betha began to invite some halfdozen cheerful young women who were related to her to sit together with them after supper with their distaffs in a quiet room. Lau came every evening in Jutta's old skirt and smock, sat down on the floor in a corner well away from the warm stove, and listened to their chatter. At first she was just a silent guest but soon became friendly and familiar with them all. For her sake Mrs Betha one evening set about preparing her Christmas crib for her grandchildren in good time: the Mother of God with the baby in the stable, and near her the three wise men from the east, each one with his camel on which he had ridden and brought his gifts. In order to tidy all this up and glue together the loose bits, the landlady sat at the table in the light with her spectacles on, and Lau watched her with great delight. At the same time she also heard with pleasure the sacred stories which were told her, though not, however much the landlady would have hoped, comprehending them fully or taking them to heart.

Mrs Betha knew several more instructive fables and rhymes, as well as subtle questions and riddles. She took charge and set them one after another in a kind of guessing game, because the water nymph was by nature fond of such things, and always seemed very content when she hit on the answer now and again (though she was not always very successful). There was one that was her favourite, and she was able to say without hesitation what was meant by it:

»I am a skinny queen,
I wear on my head a dainty crown,
And those who serve me loyally
Will have a great reward.

My maidservants must dress my hair
And tell me endless stories.
They don't leave a single hair on me,
But you never see me bald.

I go walking for all to see,
So fast and splendidly,
Yet I do not move from the spot –
Tell me, good people, what can I be?«

In this connection she said, rather more cheerfully than before: »When some time in the future I am in my homeland again, and a native of Swabia comes along, especially one from your town, either on his way to war or for any other reason through the land of Walachia to our shores, let him call me by name at the place where the river at its widest point flows into the sea – for understand, my husband's realm stretches for ten miles into this sea, as far as the sweet water colours it with its own colour – and I will come and advise and help the stranger. But in order to be sure that it is I, and not another who might harm him, let him ask the riddle. No one of our race except me will be able to answer him, because in that country such distaffs and spinning wheels as you have in Swabia are not seen, nor do the people there know your language. So let this riddle be the password.«

On another evening the story was told of Dr Veylland and Count Conrad of Wirtemberg, the chief judicial officer of the district, in whose days a town named Stuttgart did not yet exist. In the meadow valley where this town eventually rose up stood only a stately castle with a moat and draw-bridge, built by Bruno, the canon of Speyer cathedral and Conrad's uncle, and not far away from it a tall stone house. At that time a strange man, very skilled in natural arts and medical matters, lived in it quite alone with an old servant. This man had travelled around in the world with his master, the count, in hot countries from which he brought to Swabia many strange animals and various kinds of plants and wonders of the sea. In the hallway of his house a great many strange things could be seen hanging from the walls: the skin of a crocodile as well as snakes and flying fishes. The count came to see him practically every week, rarely seeking the company of other people. Some people declared that this strange man could make gold. It is certain that he could make himself invisible, for he kept among his things the tooth of a Kraken. When he was once on the Red Sea and he lowered a plumbline to ascertain the depth, there was a jerk under the water so that the rope almost broke. A Kraken had bitten into the lead and left two of its teeth in it. They were as sharp as a shoemaker's awl and gleaming black. One of

größten Gütern, so man fur Geld nicht haben kann, gehört, der Doktor aber dafür hielt, es zieme eine solche Gabe niemand besser als einem weisen und wohldenkenden Gebieter, damit er überall, in seinen eigenen und Feindes Landen, sein Ohr und Auge habe, so gab er einen dieser Zähne seinem Grafen, wie er ja ohnedem wohl schuldig war, mit Anzeigung von dessen Heimlichkeit, davon der Herr nichts wußte. Von diesem Tage an erzeigte sich der Graf dem Doktor gnädiger als allen seinen Edelleuten oder Räten und hielt ihn recht als seinen lieben Freund, ließ ihm auch gern und sonder Neid das Lot zu eigen, darin der andere Zahn war, doch unter dem Gelöbnis, sich dessen ohne Not nicht zu bedienen, auch ihn vor seinem Ableben entweder ihm, dem Grafen, erblich zu verlassen oder auf alle Weise der Welt zu entrücken, wo nicht ihn gänzlich zu vertilgen. Der edle Graf starb aber um zwei Jahre eher als der Veylland und hinterließ das Kleinod seinen Söhnen nicht; man glaubt, aus Gottesfurcht und weiser Vorsicht hab ers mit in das Grab genommen oder sonst verborgen.

Wie nun der Doktor auch am Sterben lag, so rief er seinen treuen Diener Curt zu ihm ans Bett und sagte: »Lieber Curt! es gehet diese Nacht mit mir zum Ende, so will ich dir noch deine guten Dienste danken und etliche Dinge befehlen. Dort bei den Büchern, in dem Fach zu unterst in der Ecke, ist ein Beutel mit hundert Imperialen, den nimm sogleich zu dir; du wirst auf Lebenszeit genug daran haben. Zum zweiten, das alte geschriebene Buch in dem Kästlein daselbst verbrenne jetzt vor meinen Augen hier in dem Kamin. Zum dritten findest du ein Bleilot dort, das nimm, verbirgs bei deinen Sachen, und wenn du aus dem Hause gehst in deine Heimat, gen Blaubeuren, laß es dein erstes sein, daß du es in den Blautopf wirfst.« – Hiermit war er darauf bedacht, daß es, ohne Gottes besondere Fügung, in ewigen Zeiten nicht in irgendeines Menschen Hände komme. Denn damals hatte sich die Lau noch nie im Blautopf blicken lassen, und hielt man selben überdies für unergründlich.

Nachdem der gute Diener jenes alles teils auf der Stelle ausgerichtet, teils versprochen, nahm er mit Tränen Abschied von dem Doktor, welcher vor Tage noch das Zeitliche gesegnete.

Als nachher die Gerichtspersonen kamen und allen kleinen Quark aussuchten und versiegelten, da hatte Curt das Bleilot zwar beiseit' gebracht, den Beutel aber nicht versteckt, denn er war keiner von den Schlauesten, und mußte ihn dalassen, bekam auch nach der Hand nicht einen Deut davon zu sehen, kaum daß die schnöden Erben ihm den Jahreslohn auszahlten.

Solch Unglück ahnete ihm schon, als er, auch ohnedem betrübt genug, mit seinem Bündelein in seiner Vaterstadt einzog. Jetzt dachte er an nichts, als seines Herrn Befehl vor allen Dingen zu vollziehen. Weil er seit dreiundzwanzig Jahren nimmer hier gewesen, so kannte er die Leute nicht, die ihm begegneten, und da er gleichwohl einem und dem andern Guten Abend sagte, gabs ihm niemand zurück. Die Leute schauten sich, wenn er vorüber kam, verwundert an den Häusern um, wer doch da gegrüßt haben möchte, denn keines erblickte den Mann. Dies kam, weil ihm das Lot in seinem Bündel auf der linken Seite hing; ein andermal, wenn er es rechts trug, war er von allen gesehen. Er aber sprach fur sich: »Zu meiner Zeit sind dia Blaubeuramar so grob ett gwä!«

Beim Blautopf fand er seinen Vetter, den Seilermeister, mit dem Jungen am Geschäft, indem er längs der Klostermauer, rückwärts gehend, Werg aus seiner Schürze spann, und weiterhin der Knabe trillte die Schnur mit dem Rad. – »Gott grüaß di, Vetter Seiler!« rief der Curt und klopft' ihm auf die Achsel. Der Meister guckt sich um, verblaßt, läßt seine Arbeit aus den Händen fallen und lauft, was seine Beine mögen. Da lachte der andere, sprechend: »Der denkt, mei' Seel, i wandele geistweis! D'Leut hant g'wiß mi fur tot hia g'sait, anstatt mein' Herra – ei so schlag!«

Jetzt ging er zu dem Teich, knüpfte sein Bündel auf und zog das Lot heraus. Da fiel ihm ein, er möchte doch auch wissen, ob es wahr sei, daß der Gumpen keinen Grund noch Boden habe (er wär gern auch ein wenig so ein Spiriguckes wie sein Herr gewesen), und weil er vorhin in des Seilers Korb drei große starke Schnürbund liegen sehn, so holte er dieselben her und band das Lot an einen. Es lagen just auch frischgebohrte Teichel, eine schwere Menge, in dem Wasser bis gegen die Mitte des Topfs, darauf er sicher Posto fassen konnte, und also ließ er das Gewicht hinunter, indem er immer ein Stück Schnur an seinem ausgestreckten Arm abmaß, drei solcher Längen auf ein Klafter rechnete und laut abzählte: » – 1 Klafter, 2 Klafter, 3, 4, 5, 6, 7, 8, 9, 10«; – da ging der erste Schnurbund aus, und mußte er den zweiten an das Ende knüpfen, maß wiederum ab und zählte bis auf 20. Da war der andere Schnurbund gar – »Heidaguguk, ist dees a Tiafe!« – und band den dritten an das Trumm, fuhr fort zu zählen: »21, 22, 23, 24 – Höll-Element, mei' Arm will nimme! – 25, 26, 27, 28, 29, 30 – Jetzet guat Nacht, 's Mess hot a End! Do heißts halt, mir nex, dir nex, rappede kappede, so isch usganga!« – Er schlang die Schnur, bevor er aufzog, um das Holz, darauf er stand, ein wenig zu verschnaufen, und urteilte bei sich: »Der Topf ist währle bodalaus.«

Indem der Spinnerinnen eine diesen Schwank erzählte, tat die Wirtin einen schlauen Blick zur

them was stuck firmly, the other was easily pulled out. As a tooth like this, set perhaps in silver or gold and carried on one's person, possesses the aforementioned great power and is one of the most important treasures which cannot be bought, the doctor came to the following conclusion: no one deserved such a gift, he felt, more than a wise and benevolent master, so that he could have his eyes and ears everywhere, both in his own and his enemies' territory. So he gave one of these teeth to his count, as he was in any case in his debt, with an explanation of its secret power, of which the count knew nothing. From this day on the count proved to be more gracious to the doctor than to all his noblemen and officials, and really regarded him as his dear friend. He allowed him, without any envy, to keep the sounding-lead in which the other tooth was embedded, but only on the promise that he would not make use of it except in need, and that before his death he would either bequeath it to him, the count, or, if that were not possible, completely destroy it, remove it in any way possible from this world. However, the noble count died two years before Veylland and did not leave the jewel to his sons. It is believed that out of reverence for God and with wise intentions, he took it with him to his grave or otherwise managed to conceal it.

When the doctor lay on his deathbed, he called his faithful servant Curt to him and said: »Dear Curt, this night my life will end, so I want to thank you for all your good service and give you a few instructions. Over there, near the books, on the shelf at the very bottom in the corner, there's a purse containing a hundred gold coins. Take it for yourself; you will have enough there for your lifetime. Secondly, take the old book full of writings from the little chest in the same place and burn it here in the fireplace before my eyes. Thirdly, you will find a plumbline there; take it, hide it among your things, and when you leave this house for your hometown of Blaubeuren, let it be your first task to throw it into the Blue Pool.« With this instruction it was his intention that, without any divine intervention, it should not fall into the hands of any human being. For at that time the beautiful nymph had not yet appeared in the Blue Pool, which everyone believed to be unfathomable.

After the good servant had carried out all that he could on the spot, and promised to do the rest as soon as possible, he then, with tears in his eyes, took leave of the doctor who departed this life before daybreak.

When the administrators came later and searched out and sealed every little trifle, Curt had indeed put aside the plumbline, but had not hidden the purse, for he was not one of the cleverest of fellows. So he had to leave it there and never saw a single penny of its contents. Indeed the despicable heirs barely managed to pay him his year's wages.

He had a premonition of such misfortune too when he arrived at his hometown with his little bundle, already sad enough in any case. Now his only thought above all else was to carry out his master's order. Because he had not been there for twenty-three years he didn't know any of the people he met, and though he nevertheless said good evening to one after another, nobody answered him. The people looked round in surprise when he came past, wondering who might have greeted them, for nobody could see the man. The reason for this was that the plumbline in his bundle was hanging from his left shoulder. On another occasion, when it was on the right side, he was seen by everyone. But he said to himself: »In my young days the people of Blaubeuren were not so rude!«

At the Blue Pool he found his cousin, the rope-maker, at work with his son, spinning tow from his apron as he walked backwards along the monastery wall, and in addition the boy plaited the rope with his wheel. »Hello there, cousin rope-maker«, cried Curt, slapping him on the shoulder. The ropemaker looked round, his face pale, dropped his work and ran as fast as his legs would carry him. Then Curt laughed, saying: »Upon my soul, he thinks I'm a ghost! I'm sure it's been reported here that I have died, instead of my master – good heavens!«

Now he went to the pond, untied his bundle and took out the plumbline. Then it occurred to him that he would after all like to know whether it was true that the pool really was bottomless (he would like to have been a bit of an expert on the curiosities of nature, like his master), and because he had previously seen three long, strong cords in the ropemaker's basket, he took them out and tied the lead to one of them. There was just then quite a large quantity of newly hollowed out tree trunks in the water, out to the middle of the pond, on which he could walk safely. So he lowered the weight, always measuring off a length of cord on his outstretched arm, reckoning three such lengths to be a fathom and counting out aloud: »1 fathom, 2 fathoms, 3, 4, 5, 6, 7, 8, 9, 10.« Then the first cord came to an end and he had to tie the second one to it. He measured again and counted up to 20. That was the end of the second cord.

»Heavens above, what a depth!« So he tied the third length to the end of the rope he had already lowered and continued counting: »21, 22, 23, 24 – damn it all, my arm's beginning to ache! – 25, 26, 27, 28, 29, 30 – Well, that's it, the line's too short to reach the bottom. There's noth-

Lau hinüber, welche lächelte; denn freilich wußte sie am besten, wie es gegangen war mit dieser Messerei; doch sagten beide nichts. Dem Leser aber soll es unverhalten sein.

Die schöne Lau lag jenen Nachmittag auf dem Sand in der Tiefe, und, ihr zu Füßen, eine Kammerjungfrau, Aleila, welche ihr die liebste war, beschnitte ihr in guter Ruh die Zehen mit einer goldenen Schere, wie von Zeit zu Zeit geschah.

Da kam hernieder langsam aus der klaren Höh ein schwarzes Ding, als wie ein Kegel, dess' sich im Anfang beide sehr verwunderten, bis sie erkannten, was es sei. Wie nun das Lot mit neunzig Schuh den Boden rührte, da ergriff die scherzlustige Zofe die Schnur und zog gemach mit beiden Händen, zog und zog, so lang, bis sie nicht mehr nachgab. Alsdann nahm sie geschwind die Schere und schnitt das Lot hinweg, erlangte einen dicken Zwiebel, der war erst gestern in den Topf gefallen und war fast eines Kinderkopfes groß, und band ihn bei dem grünen Schossen an die Schnur, damit der Mann erstaune, ein ander Lot zu finden, als das er ausgeworfen. Derweile aber hatte die schöne Lau den Krackenzahn im Blei mit Freuden und Verwunderung entdeckt. Sie wußte seine Kraft gar wohl, und ob zwar für sich selbst die Wasserweiber oder -männer nicht viel darnach fragen, so gönnen sie den Menschen doch so großen Vorteil nicht, zumalen sie das Meer und was sich darin findet von Anbeginn als ihren Pacht und Lehn ansprechen. Deswegen denn die schöne Lau mit dieser ungefähren Beute sich dereinst, wenn sie zu Hause käme, beim alten Nix, ihrem Gemahl, Lobs zu erholen hoffte. Doch wollte sie den Mann, der oben stund, nicht lassen ohn Entgelt, nahm also alles, was sie eben auf dem Leibe hatte, nämlich die schöne Perlenschnur an ihrem Hals, schlang selbe um den großen Zwiebel, gerade als er sich nunmehr erhob; und daran war es nicht genug: sie hing zuteuerst auch die goldne Schere noch daran und sah mit hellem Aug, wie das Gewicht hinaufgezogen ward. Die Zofe aber, neubegierig, wie sich das Menschenkind dabei gebärde, stieg hinter dem Lot in die Höhe und weidete sich zwo Spannen unterhalb dem Spiegel an des Alten Schreck und Verwirrung. Zuletzt fuhr sie mit ihren beiden aufgehobenen Händen ein maler viere in der Luft herum, die weißen Finger als zu einem Fächer oder Wadel ausgespreizt. Es waren aber schon zuvor auf des Vetters Seilers Geschrei viel Leute aus der Stadt herausgekommen, die standen um den Blautopf her und sahn dem Abenteuer zu, bis wo die grausigen Hände erschienen; da stob mit eins die Menge voneinander und entrann.

Der alte Diener aber war von Stund an irrsch im Kopf ganzer sieben Tage und sah der Lau ihre Geschenke gar nicht an, sondern saß da, bei seinem Vetter, hinterm Ofen, und sprach des Tags wohl hundertmal ein altes Sprüchlein vor sich hin, von welchem kein Gelehrter in ganz Schwabenland Bescheid zu geben weiß, woher und wie oder wann erstmals es unter die Leute gekommen. Denn von ihm selber hatte es der Alte nicht; man gab es lang vor seiner Zeit, gleichwie noch heutigestags, den Kindern scherzweis auf, wer es ganz hurtig nacheinander ohne Tadel am öftesten hersagen könne; und lauten die Worte:

»'s leit a Klötzle Blei glei bei Blaubeura, glei bei Blaubeura leit a Klötzle Blei.«

Die Wirtin nannt es einen rechten Leirenbendel und sagte: »Wer hätte auch den mindesten Verstand da drin gesucht, geschweige eine Prophezeiung!«

Als endlich der Curt mit dem siebenten Morgen seine gute Besinnung wiederfand und ihm der Vetter die kostbaren Sachen darwies, so sein rechtliches Eigentum wären, da schmunzelte er doch, tat sie in sicheren Verschluß und ging mit des Seilers zu Rat, was damit anzufangen. Sie achteten alle fürs beste, er reise mit Perlen und Schere gen Stuttgart, wo eben Graf Ludwig sein Hoflager hatte, und biete sie demselben an zum Kauf. So tat er denn. Der hohe Herr war auch nicht karg und gleich bereit, so seltene Zier nach Schätzung eines Meisters für seine Frau zu nehmen; nur als er von dem Alten hörte, wie er dazu gekommen, fuhr er auf und drehte sich voll Ärger auf dem Absatz um, daß ihm der Wunderzahn verloren sei. Ihm war vordem etwas von diesem kund geworden, und hatte er dem Doktor, bald nach Herrn Conrads Hintritt, seines Vaters, sehr darum angelegen, doch umsonst.

Dies war nun die Geschichte, davon die Spinnerinnen damals plauderten. Doch ihnen war das Beste daran unbekannt. Eine Gevatterin, so auch mit ihrer Kunkel unter ihnen saß, hätte noch gar gern gehört, ob wohl die schöne Lau das Lot noch habe, auch was sie damit tue? und redte so von weitem darauf hin; da gab Frau Betha ihr nach ihrer Weise einen kleinen Stich und sprach zur Lau: »Ja, gelt, jetzt macht Ihr Euch bisweilen unsichtbar, geht herum in den Häusern und guckt den Weibern in die Töpfe, was sie zu Mittag kochen? Eine schöne Sach um so ein Lot für fürwitzige Leute!«

Inmittelst fing der Dirnen eine an, halblaut das närrische Gesetzlein herzusagen; die ändern taten ein gleiches, und jede wollt es besser können, und keine brachte es zum dritten oder viertenmal glatt aus dem Mund; dadurch gab es viel Lachen. Zum letzten mußte es die schöne Lau probieren, die Jutta ließ ihr keine Ruh. Sie wurde

ing more I can do.« Before pulling it up he tied the cord around the wood on which he was standing to have a little rest, and came to the conclusion that the pond really was bottomless. As one of the spinners was telling this tale, the landlady cast a sly glance at Lau who was smiling, for of course she knew better than anyone what had occurred in this measuring. Neither of them said anything, but all will be revealed to the reader.

That afternoon the beautiful Lau was lying on the sand at the bottom of the pond. At her feet, Aleila, who was her favourite chambermaid, was quietly cutting her toenails with a golden scissors, as she did from time to time.

Then down from the clear surface came something black and cone shaped, which greatly surprised them both, until they recognised what it was. As the ninety-foot long plumbline touched the bottom, the playful maid grabbed the cord and slowly pulled with both hands. She pulled and pulled until it wouldn't budge any further. Then she quickly took the scissors, cut off the lead, and got hold of a large onion which had dropped into the pond only the day before. It was almost as big as a child's head, and she tied it by its green shoots to the cord, so that the man would be astonished to find a different plumbline from the one he had thrown out. In the meantime, however, the beautiful nymph had with joy and amazement discovered the Kraken tooth in the lead. She knew of its power, and although there is no great call for it amongst water sprites, male or female, for their own purposes, they nevertheless do not like to give such a great advantage to humans, especially as they have always regarded the sea and everything in it as rightfully theirs. So the beautiful Lau hoped one day, when she came home with what she thought a great treasure, to be praised by her husband, the old sprite. However, she didn't want the man who was standing up above to go unrewarded, so she took everything that she had on her, namely the beautiful pearl necklace that she had round her neck, and wound it round the large onion just at the moment when it was rising to the surface. Even that was in her opinion not enough. She even hung the gold scissors on the line and watched clear-eyed as the weight was pulled up. The maid, however, curious to see how the human being would react, rose up behind the line, and two handspans below the surface gloated over the old man's fear and confusion. Finally she moved her raised hands about in the air four times, her white fingers splayed like a fan or a feather duster. But many people had already come from the town on hearing the ropemaker's shouts, and now they stood around the Blue Pool watching this adventure until the gruesome hands appeared. Then the crowd dispersed and fled as one man.

From that moment however the old servant was out of his wits for the next seven days and did not glance at Lau's gifts. He merely sat behind the stove at his cousin's house repeating to himself at least a hundred times a day an old rhyme. Not one scholar in all Swabia was able to say whence or how or when it first became current. For the old man had not composed it himself. Long before his time it was jokingly set to children, as it still is today, to see who could say it quite quickly and most often without any mistakes. The words are:

»There lies a lump of lead
right near Blaubeuren,
Right near Blaubeuren lies a lump of lead.«

The landlady described it as a boring, monotonous verse and said: »Who would have looked for the least bit of sense in that, let alone a prophecy!«

When Curt finally came to his senses again on the seventh morning, and his cousin showed him the precious things which were now his legal property, he smiled, wrapped them up securely and asked the ropemaker's advice as to what he should do with them. They all thought it best that he should travel with the pearls and scissors to Stuttgart, where Count Ludwig had his temporary residence, and offer to sell them to him. This he did, and the noble lord was not miserly, but quite prepared to buy such rare adornments for his wife at a price estimated by a master jeweller. Only when he heard from the old man how he had come by them did he fly into a rage and turn on his heel, fall of anger that he had been deprived of the magic tooth. He had previously gathered some knowledge about it and had pestered the doctor a great deal after the death of his father, Lord Conrad, but to no avail.

This then was the story about which the spinners were chatting. But the best part of it was unknown to them. One of the women who was sitting amongst them with her distaff would have liked to know whether Lau still had the sounding lead and what she was going to do with it. She asked the question quite casually. Mrs Betha gave her a hint in her usual manner to say no more and said to Lau: »Yes, now you can make yourself invisible occasionally and go round the houses and peep into the women's saucepans to see what they're cooking for lunch. This sounding lead business is bound to interest inquisitive people!«

In the midst of all this one of the women began to recite the silly verse. The others did the same, each one wanting to improve upon the oth-

Doch wollte sie den Mann, der oben stund, nicht lassen ohn Entgelt, nahm also alles, was sie eben auf dem Leibe hatte, nämlich die schöne Perlenschnur an ihrem Hals, schlang selbe um den großen Zwiebel, gerade als er sich nunmehr erhob ...

However, she didn't want the man who was standing up above to go unrewarded, so she took everything that she had on her, namely the beautiful pearl necklace that she had round her neck, and wound it round the large onion just at the moment when it was rising to the surface.

»'s leit a Klötzle Blei glei bei Blaubeura, glei bei Blaubeura leit a Klötzle Blei.«

»There lies a lump of lead right near Blaubeuren, Right near Blaubeuren lies a lump of lead.«

rot bis an die Schläfe, doch hüb sie an und klüglicherweise gar langsam:

»'s leit a Klötzle Blei glei bei Blaubeura.«

Die Wirtin rief ihr zu, so sei es keine Kunst, es müsse gehen wie geschmiert! Da nahm sie ihren Anlauf frisch hinweg, kam auch alsbald vom Pfad ins Stoppelfeld, fahr buntüberecks und wußte nimmer gicks noch gacks. Jetzt, wie man denken kann, gab es Gelächter einer Stuben voll, das hättet ihr nur hören sollen, und mitten draus hervor der schönen Lau ihr Lachen, so hell wie ihre Zähne, die man alle sah!

Doch unversehens, mitten in dieser Fröhlichkeit und Lust, begab sich ein mächtiges Schrekken. Der Sohn vom Haus, der Wirt, – er kam gerade mit dem Wagen heim von Sonderbuch und fand die Knechte verschlafen im Stall – sprang hastig die Stiege herauf, rief seine Mutter vor die Tür und sagte, daß es alle hören konnten: »Um Gottes willen, schickt die Lau nach Haus! Hört Ihr denn nicht im Städtlein den Lärm? der Blautopf leert sich aus, die untere Gasse ist schon unter Wasser, und in dem Berg am Gumpen ist ein Getös und Rollen, als wenn die Sündflut käme!« – Indem er noch so sprach, tat innen die Lau einen Schrei: »Das ist der König, mein Gemahl, und ich bin nicht daheim!« – Hiermit fiel sie von ihrem Stuhl sinnlos zu Boden, daß die Stube zitterte. Der Sohn war wieder fort, die Spinnerinnen liefen jammernd heim mit ihren Rocken, die andern aber wußten nicht, was anzufangen mit der armen Lau, welche wie tot dalag. Eins machte ihr die Kleider auf, ein anderes strich sie an, das dritte riß die Fenster auf, und schafften doch alle miteinander nichts.

Da streckte unverhofft der lustige Koch den Kopf zur Tür herein, sprechend: »Ich hab mirs eingebildet, sie wär bei euch! Doch, wie ich sehe, gehts nicht allzu lustig her. Macht, daß die Ente in das Wasser kommt, so wird sie schwimmen!« – »Du hast gut reden!« sprach die Mutter mit Beben; »hat man sie auch im Keller und im Brunnen, kann sie sich unten nicht den Hals abstürzen im Geklüft?« – »Was Keller!« rief der Sohn; »was Brunnen! das geht ja freilich nicht – laßt mich nur machen! Not kennt kein Gebot – ich trag sie in den Blautopf.« – Und damit nahm er, als ein starker Kerl, die Wasserfrau auf seine Arme. »Komm, Jutta – nicht heulen! – geh mir voran mit der Latern.« – »In Gottes Namen!« sagte die Wirtin; »doch nehmt den Weg hinten herum durch die Gärten: es wimmelt die Straße mit Leuten und Lichtern.« – »Der Fisch hat sein Gewicht!« sprach er im Gehn, schritt aber festen Tritts die Stiege hinunter, dann über den Hof und links und rechts, zwischen Hecken und Zäunen hindurch.

Am Gumpen fanden sie das Wasser schon merklich gefallen, gewahrten aber nicht, wie die drei Zofen, mit den Köpfen dicht unter dem Spiegel, ängstlich hin und wieder schwammen, nach ihrer Frau ausschauend. Das Mädchen stellte die Laterne hin, der Koch entledigte sich seiner Last, indem er sie behutsam mit dem Rücken an den Kürbishügel lehnte. Da raunte ihm sein eigener Schalk ins Ohr: wenn du sie küßtest, freute dichs dein Leben lang, und könntest du doch sagen, du habest einmal eine Wasserfrau geküßt. Und eh er es recht dachte, wars geschehen. Da löschte ein Schuck Wasser aus dem Topf das Licht urplötzlich aus, daß es stichdunkel war umher, und tat es dann nicht anders, als wenn ein ganz halb Dutzend nasser Hände auf ein paar kernige Backen fiel' und wo es sonst hintraf. Die Schwester rief: »Was gibt es denn?« – »Maulschellen, heißt mans hier herum!« sprach er; »ich hätte nicht gedacht, daß sie am Schwarzen Meer sottige Ding auch kenneten!« – Dies sagend, stahl er sich eilends davon, doch weil es vom Widerhall drüben am Kloster auf Mauern und Dächern und Wänden mit Maulschellen brazzelte, stund er bestürzt, wußte nicht recht wohin, denn er glaubte den Feind vorn und hinten. (Solch einer Witzung brauchte es, damit er sich des Mundes nicht berühme, den er geküßt, unwissend zwar, dass er es müssen tun, der schönen Lau zum Heil.)

Inwährend diesem argen Lärm nun hörte man die Fürstin in ihrem Ohnmachtschlaf so innig lachen, wie sie damals im Traum getan, wo sie den Abt sah springen. Der Koch vernahm es noch von weitem, und ob ers schon auf sich zog, und mit Grund, erkannte er doch gern daraus, daß es nicht weiter Not mehr habe mit der Frau.

Bald kam mit guter Zeitung auch die Jutta heim, die Kleider, den Rock und das Leibchen im Arm, welche die schöne Lau zum letzten mal heut am Leibe gehabt. Von ihren Kammerjungfern, die sie am Topf in Beisein des Mädchens empfingen, erfuhr sie gleich zu ihrem großen Trost, der König sei noch nicht gekommen, doch mög es nicht mehr lang anstehn, die große Wasserstraße sei schon angefüllt. Dies nämlich war ein breiter hoher Felsenweg, tief unterhalb den menschlichen Wohnstätten, schön grad und eben mitten durch den Berg gezogen, zwo Meilen lang von da bis an die Donau, wo des alten Nixen Schwester ihren Fürstensitz hatte. Derselben waren viele Flüsse, Bäche, Quellen dieses Gaus dienstbar; die schwellten, wenn das Aufgebot an sie erging, besagte Straße in gar kurzer Zeit so hoch mit ihren Wassern, daß sie mit allem Seegetier, Meerrossen und Wagen füglich befahren werden mochte, welches bei festlicher Gelegenheit zuweilen als ein schönes Schaugepräng mit vielen Fackeln und Musik von Hörnern und Pauken geschah.

er and none of them managing to say it three or four times without making it mistake. This led to a great deal of laughter. Finally Jutta gave the beautiful nymph no peace until she too made an attempt. She blushed to the roots of her hair, but she wisely started off quite slowly:

»There lies a lump of lead
right near Blaubeuren.«

The landlady told her it was no great feat to say it like that; it had to go like clockwork! So she started all over again, but she immediately fell from the frying pan into the fire. She got completely confused and couldn't say a word. Now, as one can imagine, the room was full of laughter. You should have heard it! And from the middle of it all came the water nymph's laughter, as bright as her teeth which everyone could see. But unexpectedly, in the midst of all this happiness and joy, they had a great shock.

The son of the house who managed the inn had just come home from Sonderbuch with his cart and found the servants asleep in the stable. He came running up the staircase, called his mother to the door, and said in a voice that everyone could hear: »For God's sake, send the nymph home! Can't you hear the noise in the town? The Blue Pool has overflowed and the lower street is already under water. There's a terrible din and a rumbling in the hill by the pool, as if the deluge were coming!« As he spoke Lau screamed aloud from inside the room: »That must be the King, my husband, and I'm not at home!« Thereupon she fell from her chair to the floor in a faint, so that the room shook. The son made off again, the spinners ran home in distress with their distaffs, but the others had no idea what to do with poor Lau, who lay there as if dead. One of them loosened her clothing, another stroked her brow, a third flung open the window, yet all their combined efforts were of no avail.

Then the merry cook unexpectedly poked his head in at the door, saying: »I had an idea she'd be with you. But I can see that things are not going too well here. Let us get the duck into the water and she'll swim!« »It's all very well for you to talk«, said his mother trembling, »even if we were to get her to the cellar and the well, she could fall down a crevasse and break her neck!« »What do you mean, cellar or well?« cried the son. »That's out of the question. Just leave everything to me. Necessity knows no law. I'll carry her to the Blue Pool.« And with that, strong fellow that he was, he took the water nymph in his arms. »Come on Jutta, no bawling! Go on ahead of me with the lantern.« »In the name of God«, said the landlady, »but take the back way around through the gardens. The street is swarming with people and lights.« »The fish is not exactly light«, he said as he went, but he strode down the staircase with a firm step, then across the yard, to left and right, between hedges and fences. At the pool they found that the water level had fallen markedly, but did not notice the three maids with their heads just under the surface, swimming anxiously back and forth, searching for their mistress. The girl put down the lantern, the cook unburdened himself of his load, putting her down carefully with her back against the pumpkin mound. Then his own private devil whispered in his ear: if you kissed her, you would be happy all your life, and you could say you had once kissed a water nymph. And before he had time to think, he had done it. Then a swell of water from the pool suddenly extinguished the light, so that it was pitch-dark all around, and it seemed exactly as if half a dozen wet hands were slapping his sturdy cheeks and wherever else they landed. His sister called: »What's happening then?« »A slap in the face is what they call it here«, he said, »I wouldn't have thought they knew about such things by the Black Sea!« Saying this, he hurriedly stole away, but because the noise of slaps in the face came echoing from the walls and roofs of the monastery, he stood filled with consternation, not knowing which way to go, for he thought the enemy was before him and behind him. (Such a warning was necessary so that he would not boast about kissing her mouth, though he was admittedly ignorant of the fact that he had to do so for the welfare of the beautiful water nymph).

In the midst of all this dreadful noise the nymph could be heard laughing in her swoon as heartily as she had previously done in her dream, when she saw the abbot jump. The cook heard her too from a distance, and although he thought with good reason that it had to do with him, he realised with pleasure that it meant the end of her problems.

Soon Jutta also came home with good news, carrying the clothes, the skirt and bodice which Lau had worn that day for the last time. To her consolation she learned from the chambermaids, who received Lau at the pool in the girl's presence, that the King had not yet arrived, though there could not be much more delay as the great waterway was already in fall flow. This, in fact, was a wide, high rocky channel, deep below all human habitations, leading straight and evenly through the middle of the mountain, two miles long from that point to the Danube, where the old water sprite's sister had her royal seat. Many rivers, streams and springs were subject to her. When the command went out to them they filled this waterway so deep and in such a short time with their waters, that all kinds of sea creatures,

Und damit nahm er, als ein starker Kerl, die Wasserfrau auf seine Arme ... »Der Fisch hat sein Gewicht!« sprach er im Gehn, schritt aber festen Tritts die Stiege hinunter, dann über den Hof und links und rechts, zwischen Hecken und Zäunen hindurch.

And with that, strong fellow that he was, he took the water nymph in his arms ... »The fish is not exactly light«, he said as he went, but he strode down the staircase with a firm step, then across the yard, to left and right, between hedges and fences.

Am Gumpen fanden sie das Wasser schon merklich gefallen, gewahrten aber nicht, wie die drei Zofen, mit den Köpfen dicht unter dem Spiegel, ängstlich hin und wieder schwammen, nach ihrer Frau ausschauend.

At the pool they found that the water level had fallen markedly, but did not notice the three maids with their heads just under the surface, swimming anxiously back and forth, searching for their mistress.

Dies nämlich war ein breiter hoher Felsenweg, tief unterhalb den menschlichen Wohnstätten, schön grad und eben mitten durch den Berg gezogen, zwo Meilen lang von da bis an die Donau, wo des alten Nixen Schwester ihren Fürstensitz hatte. Derselben waren viele Flüsse, Bäche, Quellen dieses Gaus dienstbar; die schwellten, wenn das Aufgebot an sie erging, besagte Straße in gar kurzer Zeit so hoch mit ihren Wassern, daß sie mit allem Seegetier, Meerrossen und Wagen füglich befahren werden mochte, welches bei festlicher Gelegenheit zuweilen als ein schönes Schaugepräng mit vielen Fackeln und Musik von Hörnern und Pauken geschah.

This, in fact, was a wide, high rocky channel, deep below all human habitations, leading straight and evenly through the middle of the mountain, two miles long from that point to the Danube, where the old water sprite's sister had her royal seat. Many rivers, streams and springs were subject to her. When the command went out to them they filled this waterway so deep and in such a short time with their waters, that all kinds of sea creatures ea horses and chariots could easily pass through it. This sometimes happened on a festive occasion in a beautiful display of splendour, with many torches and the music of horns and drums.

Die Zofen eilten jetzo sehr mit ihrer Herrin in das Putzgemach, um sie zu salben, zöpfen und köstlich anzuziehen; das sie auch gern zuließ und selbst mithalf, denn sie in ihrem Innern fühlte, es sei nun jegliches erfüllt samt dem Fünften, so der alte Nix und sie nicht wissen durfte.

Drei Stunden wohl nachdem der Wächter Mitternacht gerufen, es schlief im Nonnenhof schon alles, erscholl die Kellerglocke zweimal mächtig, zum Zeichen, daß es Eile habe, und hurtig waren auch die Frauen und die Töchter auf dem Platz.

Die Lau begrüßte sie wie sonst vom Brunnen aus, nur war ihr Gesicht von der Freude verschönt, und ihre Augen glänzten, wie man es nie an ihr gesehen. Sie sprach: »Wißt, daß mein Ehgemahl um Mitternacht gekommen ist. Die Schwieger hat es ihm voraus verkündigt ohnelängst, daß sich in dieser Nacht mein gutes Glück vollenden soll, darauf er ohne Säumen auszog, mit Geleit der Fürsten, seinem Ohm und meinem Bruder Synd und vielen Herren. Am Morgen reisen wir. Der König ist mir hold und gnädig, als hieß' ich von heute an erst sein Gespons. Sie werden gleich vom Mahl aufstehn, sobald sie den Umtrunk gehalten. Ich schlich auf meine Kammer und hierher, noch meine Gastfreunde zu grüßen und zu herzen. Ich sage Dank, Frau Ahne, liebe Jutta, Euch Söhnerin und Jüngste dir. Grüßet die Männer und die Mägde. In jedem dritten Jahr wird euch Botschaft von mir; auch mag es wohl geschehn, daß ich noch bälder komme selber, da bring ich mit auf diesen meinen Armen ein lebend Merkmal, daß die Lau bei euch gelacht. Das wollen euch die Meinen allezeit gedenken, wie ich selbst. Für jetzo, wisset, liebe Wirtin, ist mein Sinn: einen Segen zu stiften in dieses Haus für viele seiner Gäste. Oft habe ich vernommen, wie Ihr den armen wandernden Gesellen Guts getan mit freier Zehrung und Herberg. Damit Ihr solchen fortan mögt noch eine weitere Handreichung tun, so werdet Ihr zu diesem Ende finden beim Brunnen hier einen steinernen Krug voll guter Silbergroschen: davon teilt ihnen nach Gutdünken mit, und will ich das Gefäß, bevor der letzte Pfennig ausgegeben, wieder füllen. Zudem will ich noch stiften auf alle hundert Jahr fünf Glückstage (denn dies ist meine holde Zahl), mit unterschiedlichen Geschenken, also daß, wer von reisenden Gesellen der erste über Eure Schwelle tritt am Tag, der mir das erste Lachen brachte, der soll empfangen, aus Eurer oder Eurer Kinder Hand, von fünferlei Stücken das Haupt. Ein jeder, so den Preis gewinnt, gelobe, nicht Ort noch Zeit dieser Bescherung zu verraten. Ihr findet aber solche Gaben jedesmal hier nächst dem Brunnen. Die Stiftung, wisset, mache ich für alle Zeit, solang ein Glied von Eurem Stammen auf der Wirtschaft ist.«

Nach diesen Worten nahm sie nochmals Abschied und küßte ein jedes. Die beiden Frauen und die Mädchen weinten sehr. Sie steckte Jutten einen Fingerreif mit grünem Schmelzwerk an und sprach dabei: »Ade, Jutta! Wir haben zusammen besondere Holdschaft gehabt, die müsse fernerhin bestehn!« – Nun tauchte sie hinunter, winkte und verschwand.

In einer Nische hinter dem Brunnen fand sich richtig der Krug samt den verheißnen Angebinden. Es war in der Mauer ein Loch mit eisernem Türlein versehen, von dem man nie gewußt, wohin es führt; das stand jetzt aufgeschlagen, und war daraus ersichtlich, daß die Sachen durch dienstbare Hand auf diesem Weg seien hergebracht worden, deshalb auch alles wohl trocken verblieb. Es lag dabei: ein Würfelbecher aus Drachenhaut, mit goldenen Buckeln beschlagen; ein Dolch mit kostbar eingelegtem Griff; ein elfenbeinen Weberschifflein; ein schönes Tuch von fremder Weberei und mehr dergleichen. Aparte aber lag ein Kochlöffel aus Rosenholz mit langem Stiel, von oben herab fein gemalt und vergoldet, den war die Wirtin angewiesen, dem lustigen Koch zum Andenken zu geben. Auch keins der andern war vergessen.

Frau Betha hielt bis an ihr Lebensende die Ordnung der guten Lau heilig, und ihre Nachkommen nicht minder. Daß jene sich nachmals mit ihrem Kind im Nonnenhof zum Besuch eingefunden, davon zwar steht nichts in dem alten Buch, das diese Geschichten berichtet, doch mag ich es wohl glauben.

ea horses and chariots could easily pass through it. This sometimes happened on a festive occasion in a beautiful display of splendour, with many torches and the music of horns and drums. The maids now hurried to the dressing-room with their mistress in order to anoint her, plait her hair and dress her in beautiful clothes. She was happy for them to do this and even helped them herself, for she felt in her heart that every condition had been fulfilled with the fifth laugh, of which neither she nor the old water sprite was to be conscious.

Some three hours after the watchman had announced midnight, and everyone was asleep in the Nuns' Inn, the cellar bell gave two loud rings, as a sign that haste was necessary, and the women and the daughters were quickly on the spot.

Lau greeted them as usual from the well, but her face was radiant with joy and her eyes sparkled in a way no one had ever seen before. She said: »My husband arrived at midnight. My sister-in-law informed him in advance, not long ago, that my happiness would be fulfilled this night, whereupon he set out without delay, accompanied by princes, his uncle, my brother Synd and many lords. We shall leave in the morning. The King is gracious and kind towards me, as if I had just become his spouse today. They will get up from their meal as soon as they have finished eating and drinking. I crept to my room and then here to say good-bye and embrace my hosts once more. Thank you Mrs Betha, dear Jutta, and you, daughter-in-law, as well as you, the youngest of the family. Give my regards to the men and the maids. You will receive news from me every three years, and it may well be that I will come myself even sooner and bring in my arms a living sign that Lau laughed while she was with you. My people will always remember you for that, as I will myself. For now, I wish to tell you, dear landlady, that it is my intention to grant a blessing on this house for many of its guests. I have often heard how you have helped poor wandering journeymen with free board and lodging. So that you may continue to give a helping hand to such people, you will find near the well here a stoneware jug full of good silver coins for this purpose. Distribute them as you think fit, and I will refill the vessel before the last penny is spent. Furthermore, every hundred years I shall grant five days of good luck, (because five is my lucky number) with each day a different present, so that whichever journeyman is the first to step over your threshold on the date on which I laughed for the first time shall receive from your or your children's hands the most beautiful of the five articles. Each one who wins the prize must swear not to divulge the time or place of receiving it. You will find these gifts each time here by the well. This arrangement, be it known, I make for all time, as long as a member of your family is at the inn.«

After these words she took her leave once more and kissed each one of them. The two women and the girls wept copiously. She put a ring with green enamelling on Jutta's finger, saying as she did so; »Farewell, Jutta. We have enjoyed great friendship together. May it continue in our memories in the future!« Then she slid down into the water, waved and disappeared.

In a niche behind the well the jug was indeed found together with the promised gifts. There was a hole in the wall fitted with a little iron door, and no one had ever known where it led. It was now open and from that it was obvious that the articles had been brought there by willing hands, so that everything remained nice and dry. Amongst the objects were: a dice-shaker made of dragonskin, studded with golden clasps, a dagger with a richly inlaid handle, an ivory weaver's shuttle, a fine cloth woven in some foreign land, and several other things of that kind. On its own, however, lay a cooking spoon, made of rosewood, with a long handle, finely painted and gilded from top to bottom. The landlady had been instructed to give this to the merry cook as a souvenir. Nor were any of the others forgotten.

Up to the end of her life Mrs Betha followed Lau's instructions religiously, as did her descendants too. There is no mention in the old book which contains these stories whether the nymph subsequently ever paid a visit to The Nuns' Inn with a child – but I can well believe that she did!